Natural Environments
自然奇觀

Joanna Burgess

Editor: Rebecca Raynes
Design and art direction: Nadia Maestri
Computer graphics: Maura Santini
Picture research: Laura Lagomarsino

Picture credits
Cideb Archive; © RICKEY ROGERS / Reuters / Contrasto: 16;
© Pedro Costa / epa / Corbis: 17; Getty Images: 19; © Micro
Discovery / Corbis: 34 bottom; Steve Corner: 38; LAWRENCE
BENDER PROD. / PARTICIPANT PROD. /Album: 53; TM 20
TH CENTURY FOX / Album: 54; © Natalie Fobes / CORBIS:
62; © George Steinmetz / Corbis: 63; De Agostini Picture
Library: 74; © Lynsey Addario / Corbis: 77; © Hugh Sitton /
zefa / Corbis: 80; RH003320 I Value RM I © Robert Holmes
/ CORBIS: 81; © Bettmann / CORBIS: 85; © Denis O'Regan /
Corbis: 86; © Liba Taylor / CORBIS: 90.

書　　名：*Natural Environments* 自然奇觀
作　　者：Joanna Burgess
責任編輯：黃家麗　　王朴真
封面設計：張　毅　李小丹
出　　版：商務印書館 (香港) 有限公司
　　　　　香港筲箕灣耀興道 3 號東滙廣場 8 樓
　　　　　http://www.commercialpress.com.hk
發　　行：香港聯合書刊物流有限公司
　　　　　香港新界大埔汀麗路 36 號中華商務印刷大廈 3 字樓
印　　刷：中華商務彩色印刷有限公司
　　　　　香港新界大埔汀麗路 36 號中華商務印刷大廈 14 字樓
版　　次：2013 年 4 月第 1 版第 1 次印刷
　　　　　© 2013 商務印書館 (香港) 有限公司
　　　　　ISBN 978 962 07 1998 1
　　　　　Printed in Hong Kong

Contents

The text is recorded in full.

 These symbols indicate the beginning and end of the passages linked to
the listening activities. 標誌表示與聽力練習有關的錄音片段開始和結束。

Before you read

1 Puzzle

In this book we will often use the words in the box on page 5 to talk about the environment. Work in pairs and use the definitions to complete the puzzle with these words. Use a dictionary to help you.

```
         1 E □□□□□□□□□
2 □□□□□□ N □□□□
         3 V □□□□□□□□□□
      4 □□ I □
      5 □□ R □□□
   6 □□□□ O □
   7 □□□ N □□□
      8 □□ M □□□□□□
      9 □□ E □□□
     10 □□ N □□□□
11 □□□□□ T □□□
     12 □ A □□□□□□□□
    13 □ L □□□
   14 L □□□□□□□□
  15 □□ Y □□□

16 □□□□□□ F □
      17 □ R □□□
   18 □□□□□ I □ □□□□□
  19 □□□□□ E □□□
     20 □□ N □□□□□□
   21 □□□ D □□
     22 □ L □□□□□
  23 □□□ Y □□□□
```

atmosphere   pollution   vegetation   recycled   crops   minerals
soil   carbon   nutrients   tundra   equator   organism
ecosystem   wildlife   conserve   oxygen   flood   latitude
fossil fuels   species   evaporation   sustainable   climate

1   An area and the animals, plants and people that live in it.

2   In a way that doesn't cause damage to the environment.

3   The plants in a particular place.

4   Plants grow in this brown substance.

5   This very important substance is found in coal and oil.

6   The line which goes around the Earth, halfway between the North Pole and the South Pole.

7   A living thing.

8   The mixture of gases around the Earth.

9   Group of plants or animals with the same characteristics.

10   Stop from being damaged or destroyed.

11   When air, water or land is made dirty.

12   The process when a liquid changes into a gas.

13   Cover land which is usually dry with water.

14   The distance in degrees (°) north or south of the equator.

15   All living things need this gas to breath.

16   Animals and plants that live in natural conditions.

17   Farmers grow a lot of these plants and their products to sell.

18   We remove these very old substances from the ground and burn them for many things including industry, heating and transport.

19   Plants use these chemical substances to grow. They are found in the soil.

20   We take these substances, e.g. salt, from the ground and use them for different things.

21   You find this area of flat, treeless land in the north of Europe, Asia and North America.

22   The typical weather conditions in a particular place.

23   Used again.

CHAPTER ONE

An Introduction to Ecosystems

自然與人

*Life on Earth is organised into
millions of different ecosystems.
They can be enormous
like the Amazon rainforest
or very small like
a single tree.*

Characteristics of Ecosystems

In all ecosystems, there are living organisms such as plants and animals and non-living parts such as the soil, the climate, sunlight and water. Some things such as water, food, oxygen (O_2) and carbon are necessary for life on Earth.

Energy [1] for life on Earth comes from the sun. Green plants use the sun's energy to make sugar. The plants absorb [2] sunlight, carbon dioxide gas (CO_2) and water from the atmosphere. They make sugar and release [3] oxygen. This process [4] is called **photosynthesis** and it is necessary for all living organisms.

1. **energy**：能源
2. **absorb**：吸收
3. **release**：釋放
4. **process**：過程

Green plants are the first stage of a food chain, in which organisms get energy from the plants or animals which they eat. As you move up a **food chain**, the animals get bigger and need more energy to live. For example, in an ocean the very small plants called phytoplankton make sugar by photosynthesis. Very small sea animals eat the phytoplankton and these are eaten by small fish. Bigger fish eat the small fish and then they are eaten by even bigger fish such as tuna [1]. At the top of the food chain there are sharks, which eat the tuna. The sugar produced by the plants passes through four stages of the food chain before the shark eats it.

The sun is also very important in the **water cycle**. Heat from the sun changes the water in oceans and rivers from its usual liquid form to a gas. This process is called **evaporation**. The water forms clouds which produce rain or snow and the water returns to the land, where plants and animals use it. The water passes through the vegetation and the soil, always moving in a downward direction. It collects in rivers and finally in the oceans, where the process starts again.

Plants remove CO_2 from the atmosphere. When animals eat the plants, the **carbon** passes to the animals. When they die, the carbon passes into the soil and after thousands of years becomes fossil fuels such as oil or coal.

The movement of water in the water cycle.

1.   **tuna**：吞拿魚

We burn these fuels for industry, heating and transport and release the carbon back into the atmosphere as CO_2. People and animals also release CO_2 into the atmosphere when they breathe. The carbon, a gas again, is used in photosynthesis and the carbon cycle starts again.

The carbon cycle.

Ecosystems and Man

Organisms have everything they need for life because of these natural processes. But now, humans have a bigger effect on ecosystems and the natural cycles than they did in the past. This is because of changes to our way of life. About 10,000 years ago humans started growing food and keeping animals in order to have food for their families and be able to sell any extra food. Cities began to develop and the population started to grow. Many years later, at the beginning of the 18th century, there was another important change. The Western World started burning fuels such as wood and coal for industry. There were many positive things about the Industrial Revolution [1] but it was the cause of **pollution**.

The world's population is increasing and so we need more food. Cities are growing and we use a lot of natural resources [2]. These are some reasons why some parts of the Earth are in danger. We are going to look at four environments which are found all over the world — forests, oceans, the polar regions and deserts.

1. **Industrial Revolution** : 工業革命
2. **resources** : 資源

The text and **beyond**

PET ① Comprehension check

Look at the sentences below about Chapter One. Decide if each sentence is correct or incorrect. If it is correct, mark A. If it is not correct, mark B.

		A	B
1	All organisms need water, food and soil to live.	☐	☐
2	Plants use light from the sun to make carbon dioxide gas.	☐	☐
3	Animals at the top of the food chain are smaller than those at the bottom.	☐	☐
4	The sun is an important part of the water cycle.	☐	☐
5	Fossil fuels are very useful for humans.	☐	☐
6	Humans produce carbon dioxide when they breathe.	☐	☐
7	Cities began to develop at the beginning of the 18th century.	☐	☐
8	The population is getting bigger but cities are getting smaller.	☐	☐

② Photosynthesis

Put the sentences into the correct order to make a description of photosynthesis.

A ☐ The sunlight is absorbed by a substance inside the plants called chlorophyll.

B ☐ Animals eat the green plants and get energy from them.

C 1 The sun shines on green plants and algae.

D ☐ A chemical reaction takes place and sugars are produced.

E ☐ CO_2 and water are also absorbed by the plants.

F ☐ Oxygen is released into the atmosphere because of the reaction.

1 ACTIVITIES

3 Speaking

Work in pairs. What can you remember about the water cycle and the carbon cycle?

Student A: describe the water cycle to your partner. Use these words to help you. Start like this: Water is stored in rivers and oceans...

> rivers and oceans   evaporation   rain   plants and animals   soil

Student B: describe the carbon cycle to your partner. Use these words to help you. Start like this: Plants absorb CO_2 from the atmosphere in a process called photosynthesis...

> photosynthesis   carbon   fossil fuels   burn   breathe

PET 4 Sentence transformation

Here are some sentences from Chapter One. For each question, complete the second sentence so that it means the same as the first. Use no more than three words. There is an example at the beginning (0).

0   Photosynthesis is necessary for all living organisms.
All living organisms **depend on** photosynthesis to live.

1   In an ocean very small plants called phytoplankton make sugar.
Sugar .... very small plants called phytoplankton.

2   We release the carbon back into the atmosphere as CO_2.
Carbon .... back into the atmosphere as CO_2.

3   Humans have a bigger effect on ecosystems than in the past.
The effect of humans on ecosystems .... in the past.

4   There were many positive things about The Industrial Revolution but it was the cause of pollution.
Although the Industrial Revolution was positive, pollution .... because of it.

5   The world's population is increasing and so we need more food.
We need more food .... the world's population is increasing.

Before you read

1 **Vocabulary**

A **Match these verbs from Chapter Two to the correct definition below. Use a dictionary to help you.**

A store   **B** adapt   **C** clear   **D** survive

1 ☐ Change.
2 ☐ Totally remove something from a place.
3 ☐ Continue to live but in difficult conditions.
4 ☐ Keep something to use in the future.

B **Now use the verbs from A to complete the following sentences. Use an appropriate tense of the verb.**

1 Some animals make holes in the ground and .... food in them for the winter.
2 Many animals don't .... when there is a forest fire.
3 Life is very different in her country but she .... to the new culture.
4 They .... the land and built houses on it.

2 **Reading pictures**

Look at the pictures of some different types of forests on pages 14-15 and talk about the following questions.

1 What differences can you see between the trees in the different pictures? Think about their size, shape and density.
2 What do you think the climate is like in each of the three forests?
3 Where do you think you can find these different types of forest?

CHAPTER TWO

Forests

參天大樹

*Forests are full of life: 90% of plants
and animals that we know about
live in forests all over the world.
They are sometimes called
the Earth's lungs because
they produce oxygen
which animals and
humans need to live.*

The Forest Ecosystem

When you read the title of this chapter, what did you think
about? Trees? Well, you're right. Trees are the biggest and most
common living thing in a forest. But millions of other types or
species of plants and animals live in forests, too.

Temperature and rain are very important for forest
ecosystems. The temperature must be higher than 10°C for some
months of the year and there must be more than 200 mm of
rain in a year. The amount of sunlight and the type of soil are
also very important for forests. They
influence what lives in and under
the trees.

Everything in the ecosystem is there
for a reason; each living organism [1] depends

---

1. **an organism** : 生物

on another. Some organisms provide a home for others such as the trees where birds live. Other organisms are food for others, such as the insects which birds eat. Together, the different organisms in a forest make the forest ecosystem.

Forests are important for both the area near the forest itself and the whole planet. Trees and all green plants remove CO_2 from the atmosphere and put oxygen back during **photosynthesis**. Oxygen is necessary for the plants, animals and people in the area near the forest. But you and I also need oxygen and we may live thousands of kilometres away.

Forests can also change the geography of the area. We have already said that soil, sunlight and water are important for the development of forests. But forests can change these non-living things. Forests and especially trees have a big role in the water cycle. They store a lot of water and therefore there is less in the air so the amount of rain can decrease. Forests are also important for the development of the soil, because the dead leaves and other vegetation put nutrients back into it.

Some of the many different species found in forests are used in medicines for people with serious illnesses. Forests are a very important resource for medical research.

For thousands of years people have used wood from forests to build houses, to heat their homes, to cook and to make paper. Forests are also important because people can make money from products such as rubber, oil and medicine.

Natural
Environments

Different Types of Forest

Forests aren't the same all over the world. The forests in Canada, for example, look very different from those in Africa. As you move north or south of the equator, the climate changes and different types of forests develop.

Boreal forest.

Boreal forests are found in countries such as Russia, where they are called taiga, and Canada. These zones are about 60°N of the equator. The climate is cool but an average of 250-500 mm of rain falls each year. **Evergreen** trees grow in these forests. They don't lose their leaves in winter; the trees must be strong because of the extreme climatic conditions and the soil, which isn't very good quality. The trees can be 30 metres high but very little other vegetation grows below them.

Temperate forests are found in areas where the average temperature is about 10°C for more than half of the year and where more than 400 mm of rain falls in a year. These forests are common in Western Europe and the USA, at latitudes of 40-50°N. The trees in these forests are deciduous; their leaves change

Temperate forest.

colour and fall off once a year in autumn. Because of this, in America autumn is called the fall. The trees are of many different heights in a temperate forest and the soil is rich in nutrients.

Tropical forest.

We hear a lot about **tropical forests** but you probably know them by the name **rainforest**. They are found along the equator. The biggest zones of tropical forest are in Brazil, the Democratic Republic of Congo and Indonesia. The climate is hot and wet (more than 2,000 mm of rainfall in a year) and evergreen trees grow there. The trees have many large leaves, which collect rain water. Very little sunlight reaches the floor of the forest so it is difficult for small plants to grow.

Forests are home to a lot of animals or **wildlife**. They too are influenced by the latitude [1] and climate and, of course, by the different trees and other plants which grow there. Different species live in each different type of forest. You can see brown bears in the boreal forests of Canada and Russia while orangutans [2] swing from the trees in the Southeast Asian rainforests. Siberian tigers live in the Russian taiga. Many different species of birds also live in the trees.

Why Are Forests in Danger?

Look around you. How many things can you see which are made of wood? The furniture? The door? The pencil you write with? And how many things are made of paper? This book certainly is. When was the last time you took some medicine? Do you know where the ingredients came from?

1. **latitude** : 緯度
2. **orangutans** : 紅毛猩猩

As you can see, we use a lot of forest products every day. In Europe in the 16th century millions of trees were used to build ships. Ships were used by explorers, traders and for war; about 600 trees were used to build each warship. Today nearly three billion people around the world need wood for heating and cooking.

Deforestation is when trees are cut down to clear the land for other uses. It is not new but the rate of deforestation has increased. About 130,000 km2 of forest, an area the size of Greece, are cut down every year. The world's population is increasing and so more land is needed for other uses such as farming, places to live, industry and land for animals. There are also two important forest businesses — logging [1] and cash crops. Logging companies cut down trees and sell the wood for many different uses. Food such as beans or peanuts are grown on cleared forest land and sold on international markets. These are called cash crops. Money is generally more important for companies than the environment.

Many things we do pollute the air. Industry, vehicles and heating in houses and offices all put polluting gases into the atmosphere. These gases can then enter the water cycle, and even the rain which falls thousands of kilometres away is polluted. This is called acid rain and it can damage and kill trees.

1. **logging** : 伐木

Evidence of deforestation in the Brazilian rainforest.

Forest fires are a big problem for forests. Large areas of forest can burn in a very short time especially if it is windy and the vegetation is dry. Sometimes people start forest fires because they want to use the land for farming.

So what are the effects of these actions on the forest ecosystem? Think back to the reasons why trees are important.

Firstly birds and all the other plants and animals that live in the trees lose their home and the place where their young grow up. Forests around the world are also home to about 300 million people; they can lose their home and way of life too.

Secondly the equilibrium [1] between the plants, animals and non-living parts of the ecosystem changes. The **climate** in the area near the forest can change. Without the trees, less water is put back into the atmosphere and less rain falls. It is difficult for some species to adapt to [2] the new conditions and they may not be able to survive. Species which are important ingredients in medicines may be lost.

Finally there aren't any tree roots to hold the soil together or the thick covering of leaves above to protect it. Rain falls onto the soil and can easily move it. Sometimes the soil becomes so heavy with water that large quantities move, for example down the side of a mountain. This is called a **landslide**. With fewer or no trees to store the water, the water goes to

A landslide destroys part of a road in Portugal.

1. **equilibrium** : 平衡
2. **adapt to** : 適應

17

the rivers more quickly. If it rains for a long time or there is heavy rain, the area may **flood**. Plants, animals and people may lose their homes or their lives because of floods and landslides.

But changes to the forest ecosystem can also influence a much bigger area over a longer time. CO_2 is one of the gases which is causing the increase in global temperatures, called **global warming**. Trees and plants remove some of that CO_2 from the atmosphere and store the carbon. If we cut down natural forests, we increase the levels of CO_2 in the atmosphere more than using vehicles increases them.

Positive Action

Humans have changed the equilibrium between the organisms in forest ecosystems and the non-living parts. This has influenced the forests and areas nearby but also the environment on the whole planet. However, the area of forest in Europe is growing. In China, too, they have planted many trees and the area of forest land has increased in the last few years.

A tree plantation.

There are a lot of organisations helping the forest ecosystems to find their natural equilibrium again. They are doing this in a number of different ways.

One method is **afforestation** or planting trees. The United Nations Environment Programme (UNEP) has introduced the *Plant for the planet: Billion Tree Campaign* [1]. One billion trees will be planted in important areas all over the world. In Britain, The Woodland Trust buys land and asks local people to help to plant trees on it. Since 1972, The Woodland Trust has planted more than 4.5 million trees.

Forests can be protected by **sustainable forest management**. In this way, trees and other forest products can be used but only without damaging the future of the forest. The Rainforest Foundation believes that people who have lived in and near the forests for thousands of years are very important to these programmes. It helps them to organise and pay for projects to help their forests.

British actress, Hermione Norris plants a tree for the Woodland Trust's Christmas card recycling scheme, London.

Big international organisations such as Greenpeace and the World Wildlife Fund for nature (WWF) also have very important and well-known campaigns. They want forest ecosystems to return to their natural state and ask **politicians, governments** and **people like you and me** to help them.

1. **a campaign** : 活動

What Can You Do?

Companies produce goods and offer services according to what we want. They want our money and so what we buy, where we shop, how we live our lives and where we go on holiday influence what companies produce and how. This can influence forest ecosystems around the world. Some very simple choices can make a big difference. Here are some examples:

- Always use recycled paper and use both sides of it. Fewer trees will have to be cut down.
- Walk or use public transport. Fewer gases which cause acid rain and damage forest ecosystems will be released into the air.
- Don't buy furniture made of wood from tropical forests. Some of these species are in great danger.
- Get involved in a local campaign. Plant trees or tell your friends about the problem and help the situation.

Remember that even if you live thousands of kilometres from a forest, your choices have an effect on the equilibrium of forests all over the world. That change in equilibrium has an effect on all of our lives.

The text and **beyond**

Read the questions about Chapter Two. For each question, choose the correct answer — A, B, C or D.

1 Which conditions are necessary for forests to develop?

   A ☐ a lot of sunlight and good quality soil
   B ☐ a temperature of more than 10° C all year and more than 200 mm of rain
   C ☐ good quality soil under the trees
   D ☐ a warm and wet climate

2 Photosynthesis is important because

   A ☐ trees need CO_2.
   B ☐ it puts oxygen into the atmosphere and removes CO_2.
   C ☐ it puts CO_2 into the atmosphere and removes oxygen.
   D ☐ the oxygen travels thousands of kilometres.

3 What type of forest is common in Great Britain?

   A ☐ tropical forest
   B ☐ evergreen forest
   C ☐ deciduous forest
   D ☐ boreal forest

4 What are cash crops?

   A ☐ crops which cost a lot of money to grow
   B ☐ wood
   C ☐ crops which aren't grown for local people
   D ☐ crops which are grown for local people

5 Which of these things does not happen as a result of deforestation?

   A ☐ The level of pollution decreases.
   B ☐ The soil loses its natural protection.
   C ☐ The rain water gets to the rivers more quickly.
   D ☐ Plants and animals lose their homes.

2 Summary

Complete the information in the following table using the information about different types of forest in Chapter Two.

Type of forest	Boreal	Temperate	Tropical
Countries	(1)	(5)	(9) ....
Latitudes	(2)	(6)	(10) ....
Average rainfall	(3)	(7)	(11) ....
Type of trees	(4)	(8)	(12) ....

3 Question words

A Scientists have recently discovered the ruins of some ancient towns in the Amazon rainforest. An interviewer asked the scientists some questions about their incredible discovery. Add the correct question words to the following questions. You can use them more than once.

When   What   Where   How

1 ☐ .... are the ruins?
2 ☐ .... did you find there?
3 ☐ .... did people live there?
4 ☐ .... big were the towns?
5 ☐ .... were the towns like?

B Now match the following answers to the questions.

A They were made with earth and had walls around them.
B Before the arrival of the Europeans in the 15th century.
C In Upper Xingu, west Brazil.
D Evidence of farming and pieces of plates and other pottery.
E About 0.6 km² each.

4 Adjectives 形容詞
Look for the opposites of these adjectives in Chapter Two.

1	cold	....	6	light	....
2	same	....	7	warm	....
3	complicated	....	8	weak	....
4	dry	....	9	poor	....
5	small	....	10	alive	....

5 Discussion
Work in small groups. Look around you and make a list of things which come from forests. Try to think of alternatives to these objects which don't come from forests. Do people in other countries already use alternatives? Can they be produced in a sustainable way?

Before you read

1 Listening
Look at the sentences and listen to the first part of Chapter Three. You will hear some information about oil palms in Borneo. Decide if each sentence is correct or incorrect. If it is correct, put a tick (✓) under A for YES. If it is not correct, put a tick (✓) under B for NO.

		A Yes	B No
1	Borneo is the largest island in the world.	☐	☐
2	There are more species of birds than plants on Borneo.	☐	☐
3	Borneo's forests may be useful for people who are ill.	☐	☐
4	There are more trees on Borneo now than there were 50 years ago.	☐	☐
5	Many people in Austria buy wood from Borneo's forests.	☐	☐
6	There are advantages of growing oil palms for the people on Borneo.	☐	☐

CHAPTER THREE

A Closer Look at Forests

走近森林

*Forests cover about 30%
of the planet's land area.
The different types of forest
which develop around
the world are important
for humans in
a variety of ways.*

Oil Palms in Borneo

Borneo is in South-east Asia and it is the third largest island in the world. It is divided into three regions, which are governed by Indonesia, Malaysia and Brunei. Borneo is on the equator and has a hot and wet, tropical climate. Tropical rainforests developed in these conditions and once covered the island.

The forests in Southeast Asia are the richest in the world with 13 species of mammals [1], 350 bird species and 15,000 plant species. 17.7 million people live on Borneo and many of them need the forests for wood and fresh water. These people understand the forest. Their knowledge can help medical

1. **mammals** : 哺乳動物

Oil palm plantation in Borneo.

researchers to find plant species which can be used in medicines. The bingator plant, for example, was discovered in this way. It helps people who are ill with AIDS [1].

Deforestation for logging started on Borneo in the 1970s and between 1985 and 1997, 85,000 km^2 of forest was cleared. This is an area about the size of Austria. Tropical wood from these forests is very popular for furniture all over the world.

But now there is another reason for deforestation on Borneo. Do you know what ingredient chocolate, ice cream, soap and toothpaste have in common? **Palm oil**. Next time you are in the supermarket, have a look at some products — about one in ten have palm oil in them (sometimes it is called 'vegetable oil').

In the 1990s people understood that the future of the logging industry in Borneo was limited because of too much deforestation. They became interested in growing oil palms for a number of reasons: the palms grow well because the climate is good for them, so they are a cash crop with a high value; there is a big, international market for the oil; governments sometimes help companies to start oil-palm plantations [2] because they

---

1. **AIDS** : 愛滋病
2. **plantations** : 種植園

provide jobs for the local people and help the development of an area. As a result, more than 25,000 km² of land is now used for palm oil plantations on Borneo. This land was once forest.

People think that the area of oil-palm plantations will double in the next 5 years. Oil from these palms can also be used as an ingredient in **biofuels**, which people in developed countries use for cooking and heating. These fuels come from plants and are more environmentally friendly than fossil fuels such as coal and natural gas. However, enormous areas of forest are destroyed to produce this fuel. So perhaps it is not so green.

Many forest plants and animals have lost their homes and it is difficult for them to adapt to the changed environment. There are many different projects to monitor [1] and help species such as the pygmy elephants and the orangutans. A Danish woman has started a centre for orangutans that have lost their home — there are about 650 orangutans there! In February 2007, the World Wildlife Fund (WWF) for Nature helped make an agreement between the three governments on Borneo to protect an area of 220,000 km² of tropical forest. This area is nearly one third of the area of the island and is called 'Heart of Borneo'. Sustainable management is a very important technique used in Borneo. The WWF checks that logging companies use sustainable techniques. Other organisations are working to teach people about sustainable management of the oil-palm plantations. They teach the local people about the ecosystem and help growers, producers and buyers to work well together.

1.   **monitor** : 監察

The Russian Taiga and Climate Control

One third of the forested area on Earth is Boreal forest. It gets its name from Boreas, the Greek God of the North Wind, because it is found in the north of our planet. There are different zones of boreal forest in different latitudes and different types of trees grow in each zone. Deciduous [1] trees grow in the southern part of the boreal zone but the forests in the northern part are evergreen. In Russia, this zone north of about 58°N latitude is called taiga. In winter the temperature can be -54° and a lot of snow falls, but the summers are warm and wet. The plant and animal species have adapted to these conditions to survive. The triangular shape of the trees, for example, means that the snow falls off the branches instead of collecting there and damaging them. They are evergreen, so their needles [2] don't fall off in winter.

1. **deciduous** : 落葉
2. **needles** : 針葉

The trees in the taiga have adapted to the extreme conditions.

The shape and their dark green colour allow them to absorb the sun's heat better and start photosynthesis [1] earlier. They have a special surface, which helps to protect them from the freezing temperatures. They also usually grow close together as protection against the cold and the wind.

The taiga in Russia covers an area of 12 million km². The Yenisey River divides the western Siberian taiga and the eastern Siberian taiga, where the conditions are more extreme. Logging is very common in other parts of boreal forests but the extreme conditions have helped the taiga. It is difficult for humans to work here and in eastern Siberia about 70-75% of the taiga is in a nearly natural state. But boreal forests are one of the biggest sources of wood in the world. They are a good source of money for the country. Sustainable forest management is especially important here because in these extreme conditions [2], the trees don't grow again quickly.

1. **photosynthesis** : 光合作用
2. **extreme conditions** : 極端情況

These forests are very important for the global carbon cycle and so the control of climate change at an international level. Enormous amounts of carbon are stored inside the frozen ground under the Russian forests. This carbon is therefore not able to form greenhouse gases. These are gases, such as CO_2, which pollute the atmosphere and cause an increase in global temperatures. But, all over the world, greenhouse gases are released into the atmosphere from industry, transport, heating and deforestation. Global temperatures are increasing and the frozen ground in the taiga zone is beginning to melt. If this continues, CO_2 and another stronger greenhouse gas, methane [1] (CH_4), will be released from the frozen ground. These gases could increase the temperatures even more. If the methane gas currently stored under the western Siberian forest is released, it will influence global temperature in the same way as 73 years of human activity.

Many organisations are involved in protecting Russian forests and some work with the Russian government. It is very important to protect trees and the carbon stored in them. Two areas of the eastern-Siberian taiga became national parks in June 2007. Now more than 1,700 km^2 of land is protected; it is home to many species of plants and animals, such as bears and the Siberian tiger and billions of tonnes of carbon.

1.   **methane** : 甲烷

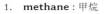

The text and **beyond**

1 **Comprehension check**
Complete the sentences (1-8) with their endings (A-H).

1 ☐ Rainforests developed on Borneo
2 ☐ They started growing oil palms in Borneo
3 ☐ Many plants and animals lived in the forests in Borneo
4 ☐ The needles don't fall off the trees in Russia
5 ☐ Boreal forests don't grow back quickly
6 ☐ Forests are an important part of the carbon cycle
7 ☐ Trees and soil store carbon
8 ☐ The amount of greenhouse gases in the atmosphere will increase

A and therefore it is not released as CO_2 gas.
B because they influence global climate change.
C when winter arrives.
D after the trees are cut down.
E because the climate is hot and wet.
F after many years of logging.
G when the frozen ground melts.
H until large areas of forest were cut down.

3.1 **2** **Pronunciation**
Listen and circle the word you hear.

1 three / free	4 ill / hill	7 fuel / full	
2 developed / develop	5 ice / eyes	8 heat / eat	
3 this / these	6 cash / catch		

Many plants and animals have lost their homes...

We use the Present Perfect in many different situations. One of these is to describe what has happened when the result of the action is important.

e.g. **action:** *They cut down a lot of trees on Borneo.*
  result: *Plants and animals don't have anywhere to live.*
  conclusion: *They **have lost** their homes.*

3 Present Perfect 現在完成時

Read the result of each action below. For each question, write what has happened using the verb in brackets in the Present Perfect.

1   There are fewer trees than there were 40 years ago. (*decreased*)
   ....

2   The local people can tell us about plants which are useful for medicines. (*learn*) ....

3   Many products in the supermarket are made from palm oil. (*use*)
   ....

4   Trees in boreal forests have special characteristics to survive the cold climate. (*adapt*) ....

5   The frozen ground under the Russian taiga is melting. (*increase*)
   ....

4 Speaking

Tell another student about a place near where you live — a park, a city, a school, a lake, a forest. Has it changed in the last few years? How? Why has it changed? Do you think it's better or worse now? Why?

Before you read

1 Listening

Listen to the first part of Chapter Four. Write the correct numbers in the following sentences.

1   More than ....% of the surface of the Earth is ocean.

2   Over ....% of water on Earth is stored in the oceans.

3   The average depth of the oceans is .... metres.

4   The area of the Southern Ocean is .... km^2.

5   The area of the Arctic Ocean is .... km^2.

Oceans

汪洋大海

*The oceans are the world's
biggest ecosystem. They are home
to some of the biggest organisms
on the planet such as whales,
and some of the smallest
such as phytoplankton,
which produce oxygen.*

The Ocean Ecosystem

The numbers 70, 97 and 3,795 will help you to understand the size and importance of the oceans. Oceans cover more than 70% of the surface of the Earth. More than 97% of the water on our planet is in the oceans and sea ice. On average the oceans are 3,795 metres deep. The oceans are therefore enormous ecosystems.

The world's oceans are all connected, but scientists usually divide them into five; the Arctic Ocean, the Atlantic Ocean, the Pacific Ocean, the Indian Ocean and the Southern Ocean. The Atlantic and Pacific oceans are often divided into two parts, north and south. The oceans around the polar regions are the biggest. The Southern Ocean covers an area of more than 20 million km^2. Its area is greater than the area of any country in the world. The Arctic Ocean is more than 13 million km^2. Does your country

World map illustrating the world's oceans.

have a coast on one of these oceans? Or maybe it is near one of the seas, such as the South China Sea, the Caribbean Sea or the Mediterranean Sea? Seas are all connected to oceans but they are smaller and usually have a lot of land around them.

Oceans are an important part of the water cycle because most of the planet's water is stored there. This ocean water has salt in it; it comes from minerals which have entered the sea from the land. When this water evaporates the salt stays in the ocean and so the water becomes saltier.

Oceans influence the **temperature** on Earth. They absorb energy from the sun and store it as heat. Ocean water in some parts of the world is warmer than in others because of the amount of sunlight in different places. Warm and cold water have different characteristics and so ocean currents [1] are created. They move water of different temperatures from one place to

---

1. **ocean currents** : 洋流

A humpback whale [1]
in Frederick Sound,
SW Alaska

another. In this way the oceans move heat around the planet. For example, the Gulf Stream is a warm ocean current from Mexico. It increases the average temperature on the west coast of Britain by 4 or 5°C. In this way, the oceans help to heat the land and air in summer and cool them in winter. For this reason, there is a smaller difference between summer and winter temperatures if you live by the coast. If you live a long way from the coast, the difference is much bigger. The average temperature in June in Rome is 14.5°C higher than the average temperature in December. In Moscow the difference is 22.5°C.

Life on Earth started in the oceans, billions of years before anything lived on land. Today the greatest variety of living organisms, plants, fish, birds and mammals, live there. The biggest are whales, dolphins and sharks, but some of the most important are the phytoplankton [2]. These very small plants produce more energy by photosynthesis than the world's forests. They are food for very small animals, which are then food for fish, which are food for birds and big sea mammals. One of the organisms at the top of this food chain is people, who eat fish from the oceans.

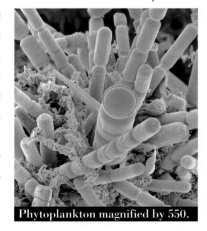

Phytoplankton magnified by 550.

We have used the oceans for **transport** for thousands of years. Today the oceans are like enormous motorways. In fact, most of the goods which are transported around the world move on ships; it is the best way to transport large or heavy goods.

Oceans are also very important for **tourism**. Many people go to the coast or on cruise ships for their holidays.

Why Are Oceans in Danger?

Oceans are full of resources which are useful to man. But this means that they are in danger because of human activity.

Fish is a very important food for nearly one billion people in the world. Many of these people live in developing countries. They use small boats and simple equipment to catch fish for their family or village. But all around the world, there are also thousands of people who catch fish to sell. For these people, fish mean money. So sometimes they don't think about what they are doing to the ocean ecosystem.

1. **a humpback whale**：大翅鯨
2. **phytoplankton**：浮游植物

Traditional fishing methods in Thailand.

A fishing boat uses the method of bottom trawling to catch fish.

One of the biggest problems for oceans is **overfishing**, when the number of some species of fish decreases enormously. This happens because commercial fishermen catch the species of fish which people want to eat because they know that they can sell them easily. The fish don't grow fast enough to replace the ones caught by fishermen and this changes the ocean food chain. Fishermen in the North Sea, for example, catch a lot of cod. This is the fish used to make the famous British 'fish and chips'. If fishermen remove a lot of fish from the oceans, the bigger fish and mammals have less food to eat. And the quantity of these species may decrease too.

The methods which fishermen use to catch fish can also be a problem for the ecosystem. One method is called **bottom trawling** [1] . Fishing boats pull big nets along the bottom of the ocean to catch as many fish as possible. But fishermen also find plants and sea mammals in their nets. But they can't sell them

---

1.　**trawling** : 拖網

so they usually throw them back into the sea. Many of them are already dead or seriously injured. It also damages the sea bottom where many species of sea animals and plants live.

International fishing laws control the species and amount of fish which fishermen can catch and the methods of fishing. However, some fishermen don't follow these laws.

Ships are used for **transporting** many kinds of goods all around the world. One example is oil, and there are many laws regarding its transport. You have probably seen pictures of what happens when one of these ships has an accident. When oil gets into the ocean, it is terrible for the ecosystem. It is very difficult to remove the oil from the water, so many plants and animals die. This can change the equilibrium of the food chain. It can also be a problem for fishermen and for the tourist industry. Accidents like this don't happen every day, but when they *do* happen, they can pollute large areas of ocean. The ecosystem needs many years to finds its equilibrium again.

Oil also gets into the ocean when companies extract [1] oil from under the ocean bed. There are about 6,000 different places under the Earth's oceans where oil is extracted. This

1.   **extract** : 提煉

An oil drilling platform at Guanabara Bay, Rio de Janeiro.

and extracting other minerals found in the sea bed can cause damage.

An amazing fact is that about 675,000 kg of **rubbish** is thrown into the ocean every hour. About 50% of it is plastic. Most of this rubbish is found in areas where there are a lot of ships and where fishermen catch fish. This rubbish, especially the plastic, is dangerous for the wildlife in the ecosystem. Many fish and sea mammals die every year because of it.

More than half of the world's population lives within 100 km of the coast. Do you? The oceans provide food, transport, trade and jobs. Think about some of the biggest cities in the world — New York, Tokyo, Bombay, Istanbul, Buenos Aires, Hong Kong. They are all on the coast. But all these people and the things which they build such as houses, offices, roads and airports, put pressure on [1] the oceans. They cause pollution and change the ocean ecosystem. Coasts are also developed for tourists.

One of the biggest problems for the oceans is the **increase in global temperatures**. Scientists believe that the sea level will

---

1. **put pressure on** : 造成壓力

Polluted sea in Cape Town, South Africa.

Hong Kong harbour.

increase by 13 to 94 cm in the next century. Ocean currents will change, which will influence the movement of many species. The temperature of the sea will increase by a few degrees Celsius (°C) and some species may not be able to survive. The ice will melt, and the oceans will become less salty. The organisms which live in the ecosystem must adapt to these changes.

Positive Action

The oceans are very important for our environment and they have a high value. We must look after them. However, some of our activities are putting pressure on this ecosystem. There isn't just one single country responsible for each ocean and so the work of international organisations is very important.

In 2002, there was an international meeting, the World Summit for Sustainable Development. They agreed to create protected areas in the oceans by 2012 and to stop overfishing by

2015. Then, in 2003, the G8 countries [1] agreed that sustainable management of oceans is necessary to reduce the number of poor people. Billions of people around the world need the oceans for food and work. But if they are not in good condition, they are not a useful resource for anyone. They must be used in a sustainable way now so that people can continue to use the resources which they offer. International organisations such as the WWF are working to help the future of the oceans.

The European Union's **Common Fisheries policy** (CFP) is important for the future of our oceans. It controls the amount of each type of fish which fishermen can catch. They must also record how many fish they catch and what species they are. It is then possible to understand how many fish there are in a particular area. Sometimes it is necessary to close an area to fishing so that the fish have time to grow.

In 2007, the United Nations Environment Programme (UNEP) started the **One Ocean Programme**. It helps communication and projects between different people who have an interest in the oceans. This programme does research and helps other international organisations to protect this important ecosystem.

On 8th June every year people all over the world celebrate

1.   **G8 countries** : 八國集團

Teen volunteers pick up rubbish from the beach during an annual volunteer event.

World Ocean Day. In 2008, aquariums [1] all over the world organised events to tell people about the oceans, plants, fish, birds and mammals that live in and near them. In Senegal, groups of people cleaned the rubbish off the beaches. In Costa Rica they painted an enormous picture on the wall to show the ocean, plants, fish and mammals which live in it. In Morocco they had a sailing competition. These events are an important way of involving local people in the oceans.

What Can You Do?

Whether you live near the ocean or not they are very important for all of you. Maybe an ocean was used to transport the oil which heats your house. Maybe you ate fish for dinner yesterday. Maybe you went to the coast for your holiday last year. Maybe none of these are true for you. But certainly some of the oxygen that you are breathing at the moment was produced by the billions of phytoplankton that live in the ocean.

So what can you do to help the oceans? Here are some ideas:

- Find out where the fish you buy come from. Do the fishermen use sustainable methods for catching fish? Some tins of tuna fish, for example, are 'dolphin-friendly'. When they catch these tuna they use methods which don't injure dolphins.
- When you are near the sea, take your rubbish home with you or put it in the bin. Don't let rubbish get into the ocean where it could injure wildlife.
- Use renewable energy [2] sources like the sun (solar power) or wind power. If we use less oil to heat our homes and in our cars, less oil will need to be transported on the oceans.

1.   **aquariums** : 水族館
2.   **renewable energy** : 可再生能源

The text and **beyond**

PET **1** **Comprehension check**

Read the summary of Chapter Four and choose the correct word for each space — A, B, C or D.

Oceans are enormous ecosystems, which cover more **(1)**...... 70% of our planet. Fishermen usually look **(2)**...... specific species of fish because they know that they can sell **(3)**...... . Sometimes fishermen use methods which damage the ecosystem and the organisms in it. Oceans are also **(4)**...... for transporting goods such as oil. If there **(5)**...... an accident and oil gets into the water, the wildlife is badly damaged. This is very bad for the people who live in or near the polluted ecosystem too. The oceans are also polluted with rubbish. Most of this comes **(6)**...... ships and fishermen. Millions of people around the world live on the coast. **(7)**...... actions on land influence the ocean's ecosystem. In the future the organisms in the oceans will **(8)**...... adapt to changes in the ecosystem.

1	**A**	that	**B**	than	**C**	of	**D**	then
2	**A**	with	**B**	in	**C**	over	**D**	for
3	**A**	them	**B**	him	**C**	it	**D**	their
4	**A**	use	**B**	uses	**C**	used	**D**	using
5	**A**	was	**B**	is	**C**	will be	**D**	are
6	**A**	from	**B**	of	**C**	with	**D**	out
7	**A**	They	**B**	Their	**C**	Its	**D**	Your
8	**A**	must	**B**	have	**C**	have to	**D**	has to

T: GRADE 4

2 **Speaking: holidays**

Many people use the ocean for their holidays. Talk about the following questions with a partner.

1   Have you ever been to the seaside for your holiday? If so, did you like it? Why/why not?

2   What do people usually do when they go to the beach?

3   What activities and sports do people do in the sea/ocean?

4   How can these activities put pressure on the environment?

3 Crossword

Complete the crossword. All the words are from Chapter Four.

Across

1　Very small plants which produce sugars by photosynthesis for the ocean food chain.

4　Part of the ocean which moves at a different speed to the rest because its temperature is different.

6　The zone where the ocean meets the land.

9　Using the wind to move a boat.

10　Remove oil or minerals from the place where they form.

11　Things which we don't want or can't use any more.

12　This person's job is to catch fish.

13　Change from something solid into a liquid.

Down

2　When fishermen catch a lot of one or more species of fish until there are very few left in the ocean.

3　On this type of holiday you visit lots of different places on a ship.

5　Move from one place to another.

7　A building where there are a lot of fish and people can go and look at them.

8　Make water or air dirty.

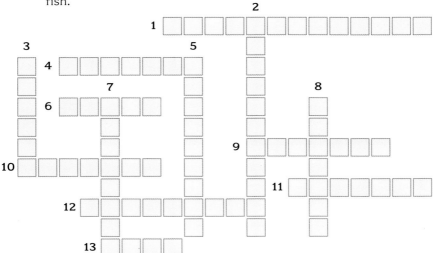

4.1 **④** Listening

PET

You will hear a radio report about an accident in the ocean. For each question, fill in the missing information in the numbered space.

The Prestige

The ship

The Prestige was longer than two **(1)**.................... .

Journey: from **(2)**.................... to Singapore

The accident

Weather conditions: **(3)**.................... .

Date: 13 November

Place: near Galicia, Spain

Countries involved: Spain, France and **(4)**.................... .

The environment

The oil went on the beaches and many birds died. Local residents and **(5)**.................... cleaned the coast.

The future

The government understands the situation better. Ships will be **(6)**.................... and more modern in the future.

Before you read

① Vocabulary

Label the photos with the words in the box. Use a dictionary to help you.

> bones   turtle   hurricane   wave   coal   shore

1 _____ 2 _____ 3 _____

4 _____ 5 _____ 6 _____

CHAPTER FIVE

A Closer Look at Oceans

深海探險

*Oceans are important for our future
in many different ways — from some
of the very small organisms
which protect our coasts
to the power which
we can produce
to light our houses.*

The Biggest Coral Reef in the Atlantic Ocean

Coral reefs are the tropical forests of the oceans. Thousands of organisms including the coral itself, fish and sea mammals live in these ecosystems. They cover 600,000 km² of our planet and are very important both for people and for the environment. Do you know what a coral reef is? Coral is made from the bones of small animals which live in some oceans. When they die, their bones collect on the bottom of the ocean and over a long time they develop into coral. It is easy to recognise, with branches like trees. Coral develops in warm, shallow water, usually near land. It forms a reef or raised area which creates a natural barrier [1]. We are now going to take a closer look at the Atlantic Ocean's biggest coral reef.

1. **a barrier** : 屏障

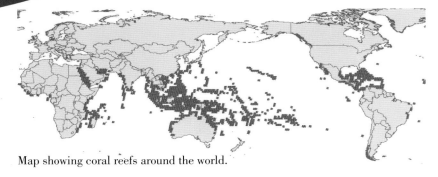

Map showing coral reefs around the world.

You can find this reef near the coasts of Mexico, Belize, Guatemala and Honduras in Central America. It is more than 1,100 km long. There are many different types of coral in the reef and hundreds of species of fish, including the mammoth whale shark. Sea birds and mammals such as turtles are part of this coral reef food chain too. At the moment this coral reef is in quite good condition. It offers opportunities for many of the two million people who live near it.

The reef is used for **commercial fishing**. Fishermen catch fish on the reef and sell them to restaurants, shops and hotels. There is a good market for these fish and so they catch a lot of them. The reef is also very important for **tourism**. People come to visit this tropical coast and some come especially to see the reef. Tourism creates jobs for local people in hotels, restaurants, shops and other activities related to the reef, such as diving.

The reef also **protects the coast** because it creates a natural barrier between the open ocean and the coast. When the waves arrive on the land, they are weaker because of the reef and damage the coast less. It also protects against extreme weather like tropical storms and hurricanes, which can be very dangerous both for people and their property.

Coral reef
in the Maldives.

The population in this region is increasing and fishermen are catching more fish to feed the people. Hundreds of ships transporting oil leave from Guatemala and pass through this area. Development for tourism is also putting the coast under pressure. Sustainable management is very important because people need the coral reef now and in the future.

This coral reef belongs to four different countries. Their governments now work together with international organisations to look after it. Local people are very important for the **sustainable management** of the reef, and the organisations work with them. These people need the reef to live and so they must understand how their actions could change it.

Organisations also teach fishermen about **sustainable fishing** methods. These methods do not damage the reef or overfish a particular species. They help fishermen to get documents to show that they fish in a sustainable way. If people buy fish only from these fishermen, then more and more of them will fish sustainably.

Responsible tourism is another important method for sustainable management of the reef. Organisations are working with local and international tourist services to teach people about their environment. The tourists themselves also need to look after this natural environment; remember that sometimes you are a tourist too.

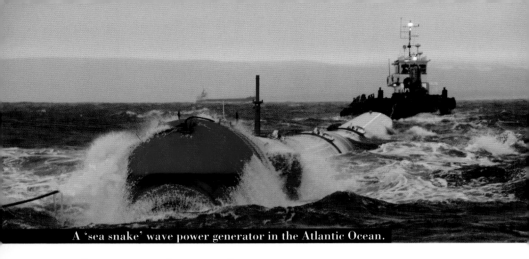

A 'sea snake' wave power generator in the Atlantic Ocean.

The Power of Europe's Oceans

About 85% of the world's energy comes from oil, coal and gas. These fossil fuels are very important for all of us. We use them for industry, cars, heating, cooking and light: they have changed our lives. But when fossil fuels burn, they release gases into the atmosphere, which pollute our planet. One way to reduce the amount of these gases in the atmosphere is by using **renewable sources of energy**. When energy is produced in this way, no dangerous gases are released. There is an agreement in the European Union to produce 20% of energy from renewable sources by 2020. There are a number of different sources of renewable energy and some of these are offered by the oceans. Let's look at two of these types of energy — **wave energy** and **tidal energy**.

When the wind passes over the surface of the ocean, it transfers energy to the water. This creates **waves**, the movements we see on the surface of the ocean. Special equipment can be used to change the energy of the wave into energy for heating, cooking and so on. There are some different methods of doing this. In deeper water the waves have more energy than at the shore, but it is more difficult to use the equipment because of the deep water.

The world's first wave farm is in the Atlantic Ocean, off the coast of Portugal. The waves there are full of energy because they travel a very long way before reaching the coast. The wave farm uses big tubes on the surface of the ocean, which look like snakes. When the waves move across the sea, these tubes move up and down and a turbine [1] changes the energy of the wave into energy that we can use — electricity. The wave farm will provide electricity for 15,000 families. There are also plans to produce energy from waves in the ocean near Scotland and Cornwall, in Great Britain.

Have you ever got wet at the beach because the level of the water changed when you were lying there? This change in the level of the surface of the oceans is because they are tidal. **Tides** are the regular changes in the level of the ocean. They are created by the changing positions of the sun and the moon and by the movement of the Earth. If you go to the seaside when it is low tide, you will see a large area of beach. When it is high tide, you will see a very small area of beach. In the United Kingdom and France there is a difference of about 10 metres between high and low tide. It is possible to use this movement of water to produce electricity.

Boats sit on the sand at low tide in Cancale (Brittany, France).

1. **a turbine** : 發電機

Rance tidal power plant, France.

In the 1960s a tidal energy plant was built where the Rance River meets the ocean, in Brittany, northern France. There is a 750 metre long barrier across the mouth of the river. As the water moves up and down with the tide, it passes through the turbines in the barrier and electricity is produced. Energy from this plant has heated homes and cooked dinners in France for the last forty years.

The oceans are full of energy and can be used to produce electricity in a number of different ways. But some of these technologies are very new and they need to be developed. We can produce a lot of energy from fossil fuels and so companies are interested in building these plants. The cost of building wave or tidal energy plants is very high compared to the amount of energy which they produce and companies aren't as interested in them. But Europe must increase the amount of energy that it produces from renewable sources. In the future we will probably see a lot more of these energy plants in our oceans.

The text and **beyond**

1 Comprehension check
Answer the following questions.

1 Why are coral reefs good for the local people?
2 Which activities are putting the coral reef in danger?
3 Give some examples of sustainable fishing methods.
4 How much of the world's electricity comes from fossil fuels?
5 Which two characteristics of oceans can be used to produce renewable energy?
6 Do we produce a lot of renewable energy from the oceans? Why/why not?

2 Vocabulary
Find the words from Chapter Five which are defined below.

1 Living things — animals, plants, birds etc.   ....
2 Not deep.   ....
3 The zone where the land and the sea meet.   ....
4 The chance to do or experience something.   ....
5 Getting bigger.   ....
6 People who catch fish.   ....
7 Person who visits a place on holiday.   ....
8 The top of the ocean.   ....

3 Discussion
In Chapter Five, we saw two different methods of producing energy from the oceans. Do you think that more energy will be produced using these methods in the future? Why/why not? What are the advantages and disadvantages of energy from the oceans? Use the words in the box and the pictures on pages 48-50 to help you.

> environment   food chain   wildlife
> tourism   local people   business

INTERNET PROJECT

Renewable Energy

Connect to the Internet and go to www.blackcat-cideb.com or www. cideb.it. Insert the title or part of the title of this book into our search engine. Open the page for *Natural Environments*. Click on the internet project link. Go down the page until you find the title of this book and click on the relevant link for this project.

Work in groups. Choose one of the types of renewable energy – solar, wind, biomass, heat pumps or biofuels – and find out how it works. Give a short presentation to your class.

Then use the Internet to find out if your country produces energy using these methods.

The Environment in Films 電影中的生態環境

In recent years people have learn t a lot about the environment and how it influences their lives. The environment has become more and more popular as a subject of films. The environment has a variety of roles in films: in some it is the victim of human activity while in others the environment gets its revenge [1] on the human population. And sometimes the story takes place in one of our extreme and beautiful natural environments.

The Victim

Al Gore was Vice President of the USA when Bill Clinton was president from 1993-2001. Gore's interest in the environment started when he was a teenager, and in 2006 he made a documentary about the environment called *An Inconvenient Truth*. He explains the real global warming situation and tells the public what they can do to stop it. Gore presents the real facts in a way which involves people so that they think about the environment and the effect that their lives have on it.

1. **gets its revenge**：報復

Al Gore in *An Inconvenient Truth* (2006).

An Inconvenient Truth was a great success and won an Oscar for Best Documentary in 2007. They are making an opera of the film, which was performed at La Scala opera house in 2011 in Milan, Italy.

In 2007, Hollywood actor Leonardo DiCaprio appeared in another documentary about the environment, *The 11th Hour*, which was made following some important events in recent years – hurricanes, floods and record temperatures. It looks at human activity in the Earth's ecosystems and what we can do to change the situation. The film includes interviews with environmental experts such as Mikhail Gorbachev, the former Soviet leader, and Stephen Hawking, the famous scientist.

There are a number of films about the effect of companies on the environment and the public's fight against them. *The China Syndrome* (1979) and *A Civil Action* (1999) are two examples of these. A very popular, Oscar-winning film was *Erin Brockovich* (2000); Julia Roberts plays Brockovich, who discovers that a local company has polluted the land and now people are very ill. She fights for both the people and the environment.

Revenge

What happens when a real situation is made into a Hollywood blockbuster [1]? The answer is *The Day After Tomorrow* (2004). In this

1. **a blockbuster**：轟動的電影

New York floods in *The Day After Tomorrow* (2004).

action film, a scientist, played by Dennis Quaid, forecasts that the Earth's climate is going to change enormously. But his forecast is too late; the polar ice starts melting and the planet's equilibrium is lost. New York begins to flood and temperatures decrease suddenly. As the film advertisement says, 'Nature has spoken'.

The Location

Extreme environments are great locations for films; they are dramatic and allow exciting stories. The African desert is the location for *Sahara* (2005), where Matthew McConaughey and Penelope Cruz have a dangerous adventure. In *Open Water* (2003) two tourists go diving on the coral reef in the Atlantic Ocean but the tour boat leaves without them. They are left in the ocean, alone apart from the sharks… *Gorillas in the Mist* (1988) tells the true story of Dian Fossey in the African rainforest; she worked there to save the mountain gorillas. *The March of the Penguins* (2005) tells the story of penguins and how they adapt to life in the Antarctic. This film won the Oscar for Best Documentary in 2006.

PET ❶ **Comprehension check**

Look at the sentences below. Decide if each sentence is correct or incorrect. If it is correct, mark A. If it is not correct, mark B.

	A	B
1 The president of the USA made a documentary about the environment.	☐	☐
2 They are using the information in the film to make an opera about the environment.	☐	☐
3 Leonardo DiCaprio was in an action film about climate change.	☐	☐
4 In *The Day After Tomorrow* a scientist is able to win against the environment.	☐	☐
5 Dian Fossey worked with animals in the Sahara Desert.	☐	☐

INTERNET PROJECT

Environmental Documentaries

Connect to the Internet and go to www.blackcat-cideb.com or www.cideb.it. See page 52 for how to find the relevant link.

An Inconvenient Truth

Look at the information on the *An Inconvenient Truth* website about global warming. Read the forecasts for the future. Which will affect your country? How? Have any of them already started happening? Now click on 'Watch the Trailer' to find out more about the film.

The 11ᵗʰ Hour

Choose one of the topics on this site – land, water, sustainable design, human impact or our emissions. Read the facts and the tips about what you can do to help the environment. Can you change any of your actions in the way that the tips suggest?

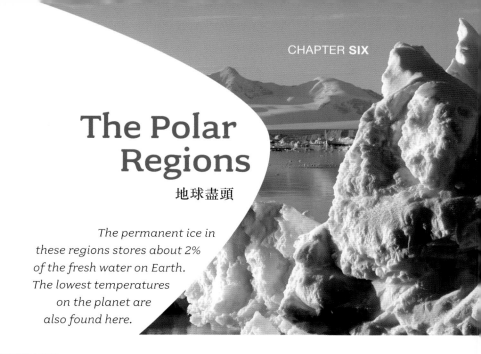

CHAPTER SIX

The Polar Regions

地球盡頭

The permanent ice in these regions stores about 2% of the fresh water on Earth. The lowest temperatures on the planet are also found here.

The Polar Ecosystem

The polar regions are the areas at the extreme north, the Arctic, and the extreme south, the Antarctic. At the centre of these regions are the North and South Poles. The Antarctic is the area south of 60°S latitude and the Arctic is the area north of where trees stop growing (about 65°N).

These are the parts of the Earth furthest from the sun. Its energy must travel a long way to get there and therefore it isn't very strong. It is very difficult for the sun to warm up these ecosystems and they are very **cold**. Most of the water in the ecosystem is snow or ice. Ice covers the surface of the land and the ocean is frozen for many months of the year. The white ice and snow send 85% of sunlight back into the atmosphere. In these regions it is permanently light in summer and dark in winter. On 21 June, when the North Pole is turned towards the sun, it is **light** for **24 hours a day** (the so-called "midnight sun"). The South Pole is therefore turned away from the sun and it is **dark** (the polar night).

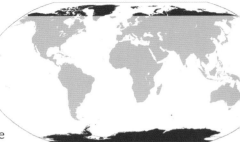

Map showing the polar regions.

It is difficult to imagine anything living in this extreme environment. But over the years some species of plants and animals have adapted to the conditions, such as polar bears, whales, seals[1] and penguins.

The polar regions are important for a number of reasons. About 2% of the fresh water on Earth is stored in the permanent ice in the polar regions. This store of water is important for the equilibrium of the global **water cycle**. These regions are also important for **scientific research**. Scientists can understand what the climate and air were like thousands of years ago by looking at ice from deep under the surface. This can also help them to forecast the future. The polar regions are also a possible source of oil and gas.

The Arctic and the Antarctic

We can use a number of superlative adjectives to describe the **Antarctic**; for example, coldest, windiest, highest and furthest. The area of Antarctica is 13 million km² (bigger than the USA) and 2% of it is covered with ice. The lowest **temperature** on Earth was recorded here, an amazing -89°C. However the

1. **a seal** : 海豹

average winter temperature is -50°C. The main reason for the very low temperatures is the **altitude** [1]. Antarctica is the highest continent on the planet; on average 2,300 metres above sea level. Another reason for the very cold climate is the great **distance** of Antarctica from other continents and warmer climates further north. All around the continent is the Southern Ocean, which freezes in winter.

Very few species of plants can live in these extremely cold conditions and there are no mammals that live on the land. There are many food chains which include a number of birds and ocean mammals such as penguins, seals and whales. But many of these migrate [2] north when winter arrives in Antarctica. No people live permanently in the Antarctic.

The average temperature in winter in the **Arctic** is -30°C. It is still extremely cold but it is about 20°C warmer than the Antarctic. This is because the Arctic is a **frozen ocean**. It is not as high as Antarctica and the ice is not as thick. There is land around the frozen ocean — the northern parts of North America, Europe and Asia. This land stores heat and so the Arctic never gets as cold as the Antarctic. There is, however, a very big difference between summer and winter temperatures in the Arctic. For this reason less than half of the region is permanently covered in ice. The rest of the region is tundra for all or some of the year.

1. **altitude** : 海拔
2. **migrate** : 遷徙

There aren't any trees on the tundra, but there are some small bushes on the flat land. The soil at the surface is not good quality and deeper down it is permanently frozen.

The less extreme conditions in the Arctic mean that a wide variety of plants can survive. Land mammals, such as the polar bear and the arctic fox, have adapted to life there. They are able to migrate south in winter when the conditions are more

Arctic fox.

extreme. People have also adapted to the Arctic conditions; they grow food in the tundra area, keep animals or catch fish, and move south when the winter arrives.

Why Are They in Danger?

The polar regions have adapted to the extreme conditions and even very small changes are a problem. The equilibrium of these ecosystems could change because of human activity. Some takes place in the polar regions themselves but some activity takes place thousands of kilometres away. Many different countries govern these regions so it can be difficult to control the activity there.

A worker sprays the rocks as part of an oil cleanup after the *Exxon Valdez* oil spill, 1989.

It may seem like an unusual destination, but more than 37,000 **tourists** go to Antarctica in the summer months. This is a lot of people in an area where there are no permanent inhabitants. As a result there are passenger **ships** and goods ships which sail in the polar oceans. The ice in these oceans is dangerous for ships and it can damage them easily. This is a problem for the ecosystems if oil or other goods from the ships get into the water. In 1989, the oil tanker *Exxon Valdez* hit the reef off the coast of Alaska. 40.9 million litres of oil entered the ocean. This accident was a disaster for the ecosystem and the people and wildlife that live in it.

Industry is another possible problem for the polar ecosystems, especially the Arctic, where about 4 million people live. Pollution from factories in the north of Russia, for example, is bad for people and can cause strange weather conditions such as ice fog.

Russia, Canada, the United States, Denmark, Norway, Sweden, Finland and Iceland have land in the Arctic. Each government decides how to manage its own area. Companies extract and sell **oil**, **gas** and **minerals** from under the Arctic. The current problem, however, is the Arctic Ocean. Scientists think that there is oil and gas under the ocean and so some of these countries are trying to extract them. But it is difficult to decide who these

An oil rig in the Arctic.

61

areas belong to, so it is more difficult to protect the environment.

In Antarctica there is no government and it doesn't belong to anyone. So who is responsible for it? Before 1961, seven countries declared that parts of the Antarctic belonged to them and many of them started research centres there. The countries were New Zealand, Australia, France, Norway, the United Kingdom, Chile and Argentina. Then, in 1961, these countries and Belgium, Japan, South Africa, the former USSR and the United States signed the **Antarctic Treaty** [1], which controls international activity in Antarctica.

Two of the biggest dangers to the Polar ecosystems, however, are people. Many things which we do every day — use cars, heat our houses and use electricity — burn fossil fuels such as oil, coal and gas. When we burn fossil fuels, gases like CO_2 and methane (CH_4) are released into the atmosphere. When there are a lot of these gases, heat energy can't leave the Earth's atmosphere and the temperature on our planet increases. This is called the **greenhouse effect**. It is one of the things which causes **global**

1. **treaty** : 公約

warming, the increase in the Earth's temperature. In the last 100 years the average global temperature has increased by about 0.75°C and the ice in the polar regions has started melting. This change in the ecosystem itself is a problem for the land and sea animals that live there because they are losing their homes. It is also a problem for people living in many different countries around the world. Think about the water cycle; when the ice melts, the water which was stored in it goes into the oceans. This is causing a rise in the level of the sea all over the world. It is a problem for many countries and cities near the coast and the people who live in them.

Positive Action

It is impossible not to know about global warming, the melting of polar ice and the rise in sea levels. It is in books, newspapers, magazines, films and advertisements and on the Internet, television and radio. One of the most important things which governments and international organisations are doing to help the polar regions is telling us about the problem. This is because *our* actions have created this problem and we can change them and if the polar ice continues to melt, we will all feel the effect of it.

Thousands of organisations work to protect the future of the polar regions. There are many **researchers** and **scientists** working in the Arctic and the Antarctic. In fact, in Antarctica

Researchers working on the most active volcano in Antarctica.

there are about 1,000; they are the only people that you can find there. These people are of many different nationalities and go to different parts of the area. They study the living and non-living parts of the ecosystem to understand its history. But the information which they collect is very important for the future of these regions.

We have already mentioned the **Antarctic Treaty**, which is very important for international agreement in the region. Forty-six countries have signed the treaty and they meet every year. In 1991 they signed an agreement to stop development in the Antarctic and protect the environment. They want Antarctica to be a 'natural reserve devoted to[1] peace and science'.

The **Kyoto Protocol** (Brazil, June 1992) is one of the most important international agreements for the environment. Countries which sign the protocol must reduce the amount of CO_2 and other greenhouse gases which they release into the atmosphere. This is the first step to help the future of the polar regions.

What Can You Do?

People are very important for the future of the polar regions. Small changes to our way of life could make a big difference to these extreme ecosystems. The biggest problem for them is the fossil fuels which we use all over the world for many different things. Why don't we try some of these things?

- Leave the car at home. Ride your bike to school, take the bus to work or walk to the supermarket. Fewer cars on the roads mean fewer greenhouse gases released into the atmosphere.

---

1. **devoted to**：目標為

- Check the temperature of your heating or your air conditioning. Do you really need the temperature to be so high or so low?
- Look for energy from renewable sources. Is wind, solar, wave or hydroelectric power available where you live?
- Think about forests too. Cutting down trees increases the amount of greenhouse gases in the atmosphere and contributes to global warming.

Cycling in the city.

A Year in the Life of a Polar Bear

Polar bears are the largest meat-eating mammals on land and they are at the top of the Arctic food chain. They have adapted to the Arctic's extreme conditions in many ways. They have a thick

coat, for example, to keep them warm. Under their coat they have black skin which absorbs heat. They have a lot of fat under their skin which keeps them warm, especially when they are swimming. Polar bears also have very big feet for walking on snow and ice.

In the winter the Arctic Ocean is frozen. But in the summer the temperature is higher and there is more daylight. The ice melts and there is double the area of land. Polar bears use land to hunt for [1] their food

1. **hunt for** : 捕殺

65

so their lives are adapted to the enormous difference between the seasons.

It is **December** in the Arctic and it is dark and cold. The female polar bear makes a den or hole under the snow and stays there for the winter. Her babies (cubs) are born there and they drink their mother's milk. The cubs must grow quickly so that they are strong when they leave the den.

At the end of **March**, it is still very cold (about -25°C) but the sunlight is returning to the Arctic sky. The female bear has not eaten for more than three months and she is very hungry. The cubs must go out with their mother to look for food. Seals come out of the ocean in this period and baby seals are born on the ice. They are food for the polar bear and her cubs, but they don't have much time. Soon the temperature will increase and the ice will melt. Then the seals and their babies will go back into the ocean.

Polar bear looks for food with her cubs.

The Polar Regions

By **June** there is more light and energy in the ecosystem. The ice is melting fast and the seals, whales and seabirds can move north again to find food. The polar bears must look for food in the ocean. They are strong swimmers but it is more difficult to catch seals in the water. More ice melts and the polar bears eat anything they can find such as berries [1] or bird's eggs. Sometimes it is dangerous because they have to attack big animals because they want their babies.

The end of summer comes with **September**; the amount of light decreases and the Arctic storms start. The birds and the land and sea mammals begin to move south. The polar bears move towards the coast and wait for the ocean to freeze again. When it does, they go onto the sea ice to look for seals. They do not migrate south and so they must get fat before winter arrives. As the year ends, the female bears build their dens and move in for the winter. The male bears stay outside but they use the hills to protect themselves from the worst of the winter weather.

1. **berries** : 莓果

The text and **beyond**

1 **Comprehension check**

Read these sentences about the polar regions. Decide if each sentence is about the Arctic (A) or the Antarctic (B). Put a tick (✓) in the correct box.

		A	B
1	On 21 December it is dark for 24 hours a day.	☐	☐
2	This continent is a long way above the level of the sea.	☐	☐
3	There are other countries near to this continent.	☐	☐
4	Only scientists and researchers live here.	☐	☐
5	There is more ice here in the winter than in the summer.	☐	☐
6	Very few plant species can live here.	☐	☐
7	Many countries have an agreement to regulate this continent.	☐	☐
8	People and animals survive the cold winter by going south.	☐	☐

2 **So they must get fat before winter arrives.**

Complete the following sentences with a time clause from the box. Sometimes there is more than one possible answer.

> until   while   before   after   as soon as

1 The South Pole is turned away from the sun .... it is dark in Antarctica.

2 The polar regions are far from the sun and so its energy must travel a long way .... it gets there.

3 The Arctic ecosystem near Alaska was polluted for a long time .... oil from the *Exxon Valdez* entered the ocean.

4 .... the sunlight returns to the Arctic sky in March, the hungry female bear goes out with her cubs to look for food.

5 The polar bears can't go onto the ice to look for seals .... the sea freezes again.

T: GRADE 5

③ Speaking: cars and bicycles

The ice in the polar regions is beginning to melt because global temperatures are increasing. This is because of an increase in gases such as CO_2 in the atmosphere. Some of these gases come from cars. If we use our cars less, we can reduce the amount of dangerous gases in the atmosphere. Talk about the following questions in pairs.

1 Do you usually travel in a car? Where do you go in it?

2 Is there an alternative form of transport available for these reasons? If so, why don't you use it?

3 Do many people use bicycles in your city? Where do they go on them?

4 What are the advantages and the disadvantages of using a bicycle where you live?

5 What is the most environmentally friendly form of transport where you live?

6.1
PET

④ A different kind of holiday

You will hear a tour guide describing a holiday in the Antarctic. For each question, fill in the missing information in the numbered space.

Antarctic Cruise

Tour Guide
You can find the tour guide in the reception until (**1**)......................... this evening.

The ship
Facilities on the ship: shop, bar,
(**2**)........................, (**3**)........................ and international restaurant.
Meals included: (**4**)......................... .
Payment accepted: (**5**)......................... .

The cruise
The trip may change because of the
(**6**)......................... .
Wildlife: seals, (**7**)......................... and whales.

7 ACTIVITIES

Before you read

Listening

Listen to the first part of Chapter Seven. You will hear about the desert ecosystem. For each question, put a tick (3) in the correct box.

PET

1   Deserts are

    A ☐ hot and dry.

    B ☐ cold.

    C ☐ dry.

2   The biggest desert in the world

    A ☐ covers one third of the Earth.

    B ☐ is in Africa.

    C ☐ is called the Atacama.

3   Deserts develop on the edge of the tropics because

    A ☐ the air is hot and dry.

    B ☐ there are no oceans in this region.

    C ☐ there is no wind.

4   What was the hottest temperature recorded on Earth?

    A ☐ 40.3°C

    B ☐ 67.8°C

    C ☐ 57.8°C

5   Which of these is not an example of a cold desert?

    A ☐ the Gobi Desert

    B ☐ the Antarctic

    C ☐ the Sahara

6   In deserts, water is

    A ☐ very important.

    B ☐ used to make rocks.

    C ☐ frozen.

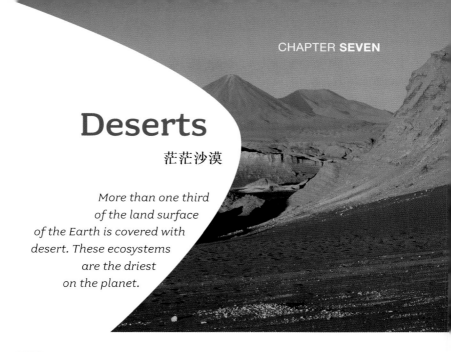

CHAPTER SEVEN

Deserts

茫茫沙漠

*More than one third
of the land surface
of the Earth is covered with
desert. These ecosystems
are the driest
on the planet.*

The Desert Ecosystem

Hot or dry — which adjective would you use to describe deserts? You probably think that deserts are hot but that is not always true. However, deserts are very dry. A desert is an area where an average of less than 50mm of rain falls each year. (Remember that forests develop in areas where there is more than 200 mm of rainfall.) The Sahara in Africa is the biggest desert in the world; other examples are the Atacama in Chile and the Kalahari, also in Africa.

The world's most important deserts are along the edge of the **tropical zone** (from 23.5°N latitude to 23.5°S latitude). This is because of the movement of hot and cold air. The area of the Earth around the equator is always very near to the sun, and the air above it absorbs a lot of heat. Water evaporates from the oceans in this region and it moves up with the warm air. But as the air moves up, it becomes cooler and can't hold all the water. This brings the short and heavy rainstorms which are typical near the equator. The air is now very dry and moves north and south, away from the equator. It begins to move back down towards the Earth, the pressure increases and it becomes warmer again. Deserts develop where there is this hot, dry air and strong winds — along the Tropics of Cancer (23.5°N) and Capricorn (23.5°S).

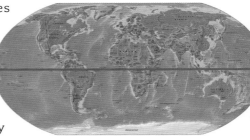

Map showing the equator.

The Sahara is the **hottest** desert in the world. The hottest place on Earth was recorded in July 1922 in Libya, where it was an amazing 57.8°C in the shade. But deserts can also be cold, like the Gobi Desert in Asia. There, the temperature in the winter can be as low as -40°C, but the summer is very different. It can be hotter than 40°C. Antarctica is a desert too. On average only 20-50mm of water, in the form of snow, falls there in a year.

The little **water** in the desert and the **wind** are very important in their development. There are very small amounts of water

Sand dunes in the Sahara Desert.

in the desert rocks. This water freezes and melts thousands of times as the temperatures change from day to night and from season to season. When water freezes, it needs more space. So, after thousands of years, the rocks are broken up by the water. They break into smaller and smaller pieces until they become sand. The wind then blows the sand around and it collects in little hills, called **dunes**. These are very typical of deserts.

Over thousands of years wind can shape the landscape but a sand storm can change a desert in a few hours. Sand from the Sahara travels long distances on the wind, as far as Greenland and South America. It is very important for ecosystems all over the world.

It is not easy for anyone or anything living in an ecosystem with very little water and extreme temperatures. But, of course, some plants and animals have adapted to them. Some plants, like cacti, have special systems so they can live where there is little water. They may have long roots to absorb as much water as possible. They may store water. Or they may have small leaves to limit evaporation of water. Other desert plants only appear when the conditions are right for them.

For animals, adapting to the extremes is more complicated because they need to always have the same body temperature. Some small animals and insects stay under the sand or rocks and only come out at night. Other animals have developed systems to survive in the desert. What do you do when you get too hot? Sit in the shade? The African squirrel uses its

From left to right,
clockwise:
an African squirrel,
a jackrabbit,
a San man
and a fennec fox.

big tail to create shade, like a sun umbrella. The jackrabbit in America and the fennec fox in the Sahara have got very big ears. The heat leaves their bodies from this large area and keeps their temperature at a safe level.

Some **people** have also adapted to living in the desert. The Tuareg people in the Sahara Desert are nomads [1], who move from one place to another to find food for themselves and their animals. The San people have adapted in similar ways to life in the Namib Desert in South Africa. They are one of the oldest groups of people in the world.

Why Are They in Danger?

Deserts ecosystems are changing. The forests, the polar ice and the coral reefs are getting smaller because of human activity. Deserts have the opposite problem. The United Nations thinks that every year the total area of desert is increasing by an area the size of Sri Lanka (about 65,000 km^2). The process by which land changes to desert because its quality gets worse is called **desertification**.

1. **nomads**：遊牧民族

74

It usually happens because of human activity but changes in climate also influence the process. When deserts get bigger, other ecosystems get smaller. Often areas at the edge of deserts are most at risk. And these areas, where there is a little more rain and some vegetation grows, are important for the desert people.

There are a number of different human activities which cause desertification. The world's population is increasing and people now use different methods to get food. They also use land which in the past was not used.

People in deserts are nomads. But on the edge of deserts the conditions are less extreme and people can stay in one place for a longer time. They use land to build houses and **grow crops**. However, the soil isn't protected and becomes very bad quality so it is impossible for other plants to grow here and protect the soil. The land can also be damaged by the people's **animals**. The wind can easily blow the soil away. With fewer plants here, there is less water in the ecosystem. This can change the climate in the local area and so there is even less rain.

Many people in these desert and semi-desert areas use **wood** for cooking and heating. But they have to cut down trees and bushes which are important protection for the soil. The Sahel is the region south of the Sahara Desert in Africa. Trees are cut down here to clear land. The trees are then burnt to add nutrients to the soil and crops are grown on this land. After only a few

A village on the edge of the Sahara Desert.

years, the soil is in a bad condition and crops can't grow. Each year, the Sahara Desert moves about 45 km south and the Sahel region gets smaller.

As you know, **water** is part of a natural cycle. All over the world, we have changed this cycle because we want water where and when we need it. In deserts too, people have changed the water cycle; they build dams [1] so that water is permanently available. Some farmers use too much water from small rivers and pools so they are dry and they cut down trees. These changes put pressure on desert ecosystems because there is very little water.

It is true that most of these activities take place inside the desert ecosystems, but CO_2, global warming, fossil fuels, cars, industry and deforestation are responsible too. The climate of our planet is changing. Many of our activities have a big influence on that change. A small increase in global temperatures could make deserts more extreme, hotter with less rainfall. **Drought** (a long period of time without rain) may become more common. And desertification may take place as it will be more difficult for plants to grow.

Wildlife must try to adapt to the changing conditions, which might not be possible for some species. And humans are also at risk. The United Nations estimates that about 135 million people may have to find new land because of desertification [2].

1. **dams** : 堤壩
2. **desertification** : 沙漠化

Positive Action

Deserts all over the world are getting bigger because of our activities. But in recent years different organisations have helped to change the management of water and the farming methods in these areas. These changes are very important for the future of deserts.

In the early 1980s there was a terrible drought [1] in Ethiopia and millions of people didn't have enough food to eat. People from all around the world read about it in the newspapers and saw it on television. Many countries and organisations gave food and medical help to the Ethiopians. Some international organisations started big projects to help the area but these were not always the best solution. Now organisations understand that small projects which involve local people are better.

Again, **sustainable land management** is very important for protecting desert ecosystems. For example, in some developing countries people now use special ovens to cook food. They work with energy from the sun and not wood. In this way fewer trees need to be cut down.

1.   **a drought** : 旱災

People using solar ovens in the Sahel region.

In the African Sahel **trees** are planted to protect the soil and to store water in the ecosystem. Trees can also be used to create natural protection and stop the soil from blowing away. In China, they have started a 70-year afforestation programme. Trees will be planted to make 'the Green Wall of China'. It will protect cities and people living in them from sand from the Gobi Desert. It will be very long, about 5000 km, but not as long as the Great Wall of China!

Other projects are designed to **manage water sustainably**. For example, water from nearby mountains can be caught and stored to use in the future. Rain water can also be collected and then used for farming, cooking and washing. And if you put stones around the bottom of a tree, they stop the water from evaporating.

Many of these solutions are very simple. In fact, one of the most important solutions is to tell the local people about what they can do.

What Can You Do?

Many of the changes to help the world's deserts need to be made by people who live in or near them. But not all of them. Here are some things which you can do:

- Reduce the amount of greenhouse gases that you produce. Leave the car at home and get on your bike, turn down the heating, turn off the light if you don't need it and tell your friends to do the same. We must stop global warming!
- Join a campaign. There are a lot of organisations which help with money and simple projects for people who live in areas where water is limited. Maybe you can do something with your school to help them.
- Take only photographs and leave only footprints [1]. Some deserts are popular holiday destinations. If you ever visit

---

1. **footprints** : 足印

one of these beautiful places, think about your actions. Make sure that they don't damage this ecosystem.

The Tuareg People in the Sahara

About 1.2 million Tuareg people live in the Sahara Desert. Many of them live in Niger and Mali in the west of Africa. The Tuareg men usually wear a long piece of cloth around their head. It protects their head from the sun and stops the sand from getting in their nose and mouth. It is usually blue so the Tuareg people are often called 'blue men of the desert'.

About two thousand years ago they started **transporting goods** across the desert using camels. They went from the cities on the southern edge of the Sahara to the Mediterranean Sea. These goods were then transported all over the world. In the middle of the 20th century the Europeans started using trains and trucks to transport goods. This was a big change for the Tuareg people.

Tourists on camels trekking in the desert.

Traditionally, the Tuaregs were nomads. They adapted to living in the extreme desert ecosystem by moving from one place to another. During the 20th century the population increased and the process of **desertification** started. The Tuareg people have had to change their lifestyle with the changing environment. Today some Tuareg people aren't nomads. They live in one place, often on the edge of the desert, and grow crops. But it isn't easy to grow food in or near the desert. Other Tuareg people have had to look for jobs in the towns and cities.

The Tuareg people are famous for their art and music. They make beautiful gold and silver jewellery and things from wood. They also use traditional music to attract tourists to the desert. For many years in January the Tuareg people met near Timbuktu in Mali. They told each other their news, organised marriages, had camel races and listened to music. A few years ago this annual meeting became an international music festival. Hundreds of Tuaregs arrive on white camels from all directions. What an amazing sight! About 500 foreign tourists come to the festival to listen to bands from Senegal, Niger, Mauritania and Mali.

The music festival increases tourism and creates jobs for the Tuareg people. Many people come from the nearby villages to sell jewellery at the festival. They then use the money to buy food. It is also possible for the Tuareg

Camp for Tuareg music festival near Timbuktu.

people to see the doctors at the festival. But organising a music festival in the desert isn't simple. The sand can be a problem as it gets into the musical equipment. Hundreds of bottles of drinking water have to be carried from 1,000 kilometres away. And the two small ferries which cross the River Niger must carry hundreds of people.

The festival is important for the Tuareg people. It reminds them of their traditional meetings and it is a sign of hope for their changing future.

The text and **beyond**

1 Comprehension check

Put the words into the correct order to make questions about Chapter Seven. Then answer them.

1 are/of/Where/the/most/deserts?/world's

....

2 things/are/deserts?/two/Which/important/for/very

....

3 Which/adapted/conditions/the/have/animals/deserts?/to/in

....

4 bigger?/deserts/getting/Why/are

....

5 people/in the/Why/burn/Sahel?/do/trees

....

6 doing/help/to/What/desert/organisations/areas?/are/in/people

....

7 1980s?/happened/in/Ethiopia/in the/What

....

8 people/some/How/cook/developing/do/in/countries?/food/their/

....

9 in/are/doing/China?/What/they

....

10 producing/Why/greenhouse/stop/must/gases?/we

....

2 Vocabulary – opposites

Look at pages 71-74 (the part called The Desert Ecosystem) again. Find the opposite of these words.

1	less	....	6	a lot of	....
2	far	....	7	wrong	....
3	towards	....	8	simple	....
4	melts	....	9	over	....
5	short	....	10	dangerous	....

PET ③ Notices

Look at these notices from the Tuareg's music festival in the desert.
What do they say? Choose the correct letter — A, B or C.

1

River Niger Ferry
Every 30 minutes
every day except
Sunday

A ☐ You can cross the river on a Sunday.

B ☐ The journey is 30 minutes.

C ☐ You can cross the river on a Saturday.

2

Camel rides to
Timbuktu €20 per
person.
Half price for
children.

A ☐ Children pay €10.

B ☐ The camel ride starts in Timbuktu.

C ☐ Only children can ride the camels.

3

Attention all visitors!
Don't feed the camels.
They can be
dangerous.

A ☐ The camels aren't hungry.

B ☐ You mustn't give food to the camels.

C ☐ Camels are dangerous when hungry.

4

Moonlight music
Every night from
midnight.
Starts Thursday.

A ☐ This concert is during the day.

B ☐ The first concert is on Thursday.

C ☐ You can only hear music on Thursday night.

5

Tuareg art store
Gold jewellery
and wooden masks
12 p.m. – 9 p.m.

A ☐ They start selling at midday.

B ☐ You can only buy things made of wood.

C ☐ You can buy here at night.

7 ACTIVITIES

PET **4** **Writing**

You are at the desert music festival in Timbuktu. Write a postcard of 35-45 words to an English-speaking friend of yours. In your postcard, you should:

- say where you are
- explain what you can do there
- invite him/her to come with you the following year.

5 **Discussion**

What do you think about the music festival in the desert? Would you like to go to it? Why/Why not? What impact do you think that it has on the environment? What are the advantages and the disadvantages of the festival for the local people?

6 **The fight against desertification**

Complete the paragraph below about farming techniques in the Sahel region of Africa. Use the words in the box.

> farmer   equipment   holes   soil   methods
> decision   organisation   food   rain   trees

Ali Ouedraogo is a (**1**)............ in a small village in Burkina Faso, about 150 km north of the capital city. In 1983, he made a very important (**2**)............ . There was very little (**3**)............ and not many crops grew so he thought about leaving the area. But he decided to stay and today he is able to grow a lot more crops than other farmers nearby. But how has he been able to do this?

With the help of a non-governmental (**4**)............, Ouedraogo started using special (**5**)............ to fight desertification. He doesn't use expensive (**6**)............ or chemicals but simple things like stones and simple tools. He uses the stones to mark terraces of land at different levels and then he plants (**7**)............ there. He makes small (**8**)............ in the land and water collects in them. Seeds are planted here and the water can go down into the (**9**)............ . The water stays in the ecosystem for longer and doesn't evaporate so quickly. The quality of the soil is better now and they are growing more (**10**)............ and helping the environment.

The Environment
in Popular Culture 流行文化中的生態環境

Popular culture is the general knowledge and experiences which people have and pass on by reading, watching, wearing, using, playing, working and talking. Popular culture often differs in different countries but with the Internet, mobile telephones and air travel it can also be international. The environment has been an important part of popular culture for many years, starting perhaps with the hippies [1] in the 1960s and 1970s.

In the 1990s people started to understand more about the environment and its problems. The environment started to appear more in popular culture and it is often used to tell people about the situation and what they can do to help.

1. **hippies**：嬉皮士

Protest against air pollution in Cleveland, Ohio (1970).

In 1970, Joni Mitchell's 'Big Yellow Taxi' included the lines,

'Don't it always seem to go

That you don't know what you've got 'til it's gone

They paved paradise and put up a parking lot.'

'To pave' means to cover with an artificial surface and 'parking lot' is American English for 'car park'. Marvin Gaye in his 1971 song 'Mercy Mercy Me' sang,

'Oh mercy mercy me

Oh, things ain't what they used to be no, no

Where did all the blue sky go?

Poison is in the wind that blows from the north and south and east.'

In 2007 music was connected to the environment in a different way. On 7 July (07/07/07) Live Earth took place. This was an enormous, international music event to tell people, companies and governments how to change their lifestyles and stop climate change. More than 100 musicians sang in a 24-hour concert in eight different cities – Sydney, Tokyo, Shanghai, Johannesburg, Hamburg, London, Rio

Spinal Tap performs on stage during the Live Earth concert at Wembley, London (2007).

de Janeiro and New York. The musicians were from many different countries. In New York and London, two different musicians sang *Mercy, Mercy Me* by Marvin Gaye. However, some people noted the amount of greenhouse gases released into the atmosphere as a result of these concerts!

British people use about 10 billion plastic bags every year. Plastic bags are a big problem because they can stay in the environment for about 400 years. In 2007, Anya Hindmarch, a famous bag designer, designed a cotton shopping bag. On the bag it said, 'I'm NOT a plastic bag'. Supermarkets sold the bags for £5 and after one hour they were all sold. People waited for hours to buy the bags at Hindmarch's shop in London and some people bought them for £200 on the Internet! All the newspapers wrote about this and it helped to tell people about the environment.

The everyday vocabulary that we use in English has also changed in recent years. *Environmentally-friendly*, *dolphin-friendly*, *greenhouse gases*, *the greenhouse effect*, *global warming* and *climate change* are all terms which we use regularly. But about 50 years ago, people probably didn't know what they meant!

1 Comprehension check

Answer the following questions.

1   Who sang about air pollution?

2   Sometimes in songs, writers do not use standard English. Look at the lines from 'Big Yellow Taxi' and 'Mercy Mercy Me' and find two non-standard uses of English.

3   What was Live Earth?

4   What did Anya Hindmarch do?

5   Why did she do it?

CHAPTER EIGHT

Looking Ahead

展望未來

*Many governments, organisations
and individual people
are working to help
our natural environments.
Their future depends
on our actions today.*

In 1900 there were 1.65 billion people in the world. In the following century, medical care improved and new methods of farming helped people to grow more food. Today, the world's population is more than 6.684 billion. Currently the world's population is increasing by 211,090 people every day. It is thought that by 2050, there will be 9.5 billion people on the planet.

As the number of people living on Earth has increased, the pressure on our natural environments has increased. But now we have something very useful which wasn't available 100 years ago. We use it to monitor what is happening and to communicate with people all over the world. It is **technology**. Radio, television, telephone, satellite, Internet and air travel have totally changed our lives. Scientists, governments and people now know more

Satellites have contributed to making great changes in our lives.

about what is happening in these ecosystems. This is very important for their future. Now many governments, international organisations and individuals are trying to help the ecosystems.

Let's look at some things which will influence the future of our natural environments.

World Environment Day

In 1972 The United Nations started their environment programme (UNEP). UNEP works with many different governments and organisations to help the environment. They want **sustainable development**. In the same year they started an event to tell people about the environment. Every year on 5 June World Environment Day is celebrated. Each year it is in a different city and there is a different theme [1].

The event involves politicians and the public in the future of our planet. In 2008, World Environment Day was in New Zealand. The theme was reducing the amount of carbon which is released into the atmosphere. As we have seen, this is one of the causes of global warming. This is a danger for all of the ecosystems we have looked at and so it is very important for their future. Three of the themes over the last five years have been about the ecosystems in this book. In 2004 it was the oceans, in 2006 deserts and desertification, and in 2007 the polar regions.

---

1.   **a theme** : 主題

The Kyoto Protocol [1]

The Kyoto Protocol is very important for the future of our planet. It was agreed in 1997 in Kyoto, Japan. By February 2005, more than 55 countries had signed the agreement. The agreement aims to **reduce greenhouse gases** and therefore reduce global warming. But how?

The protocol is different for developed and developing countries. For more than 100 years, developed countries have released greenhouse gases such as CO_2 into the atmosphere. Industry, power generation, cars and heating all burn fossil fuels and this creates greenhouse gases. All developed countries that have signed the protocol must reduce global levels of greenhouse gases. The global target is for the level in 2012 to be 5.2% less than the level in 1990. Each country has its own targets so that the global target is reached. Japan, for example must reduce its level of these gases by 6% and the United Kingdom by 8%.

Developing countries burn fewer fossil fuels and so they produce fewer greenhouse gases. The protocol doesn't give them targets to reduce greenhouse gases. When they develop projects which reduce the amount of greenhouse gases they receive

1. **a protocol**：協議

The use of solar panels in Kenya helps to reduce the amount of greenhouse gases.

financial help for other sustainable development projects. Some examples of projects are those which use solar power or stop deforestation.

The environment is international and the Kyoto Protocol is an international agreement. It is one of the agreements which will influence our natural environments in the years to come.

Carbon Footprint

Have you ever thought about how **your lifestyle** influences the environment? For example, do you usually have a bath or a shower? Do you walk or use a car? What do you eat? A carbon footprint is the amount of CO_2 in the air because of actions like these which a person does over a period of one year. When you walk on a beach you leave footprints in the sand. Your actions during your life leave a carbon footprint on Earth.

Carbon footprints can be calculated for individuals, families, companies or countries. In this way people and organisations can understand the influence of their actions on the global environment. And both individuals and companies must change their actions for countries to meet their Kyoto targets.

Some ecosystems are in danger because of the actions of our increasing population. However the future looks positive for a number of reasons: we have technology to help us to monitor the situation and change things for the better; our environment is very resilient [1]; and millions of people all over the world care about the environment and want to help it. We are very lucky to have the opportunity of improving our planet for future generations.

1. **resilient**：能復原

The text and **beyond**

PET **1** **Comprehension check**

Look at the sentences below about Chapter Eight. Decide if each sentence is correct or incorrect. If it is correct, mark A. If it is not correct, mark B.

		A	B
1	The population increased in the 20th century because there were many farms.	☐	☐
2	There is more pressure on our ecosystems because there are more people on Earth.	☐	☐
3	Technology has always been important for our ecosystems.	☐	☐
4	Developing countries pollute the air more than developed countries.	☐	☐
5	Everyone's way of life has an effect on the environment.	☐	☐
6	Companies must calculate their carbon footprint because of the Kyoto Protocol.	☐	☐

In 1900 there were 1.65 billion people in the world.

In English we say different types of numbers in different ways:

In the 21st century, we have changed the way to say **years**

e.g.   *1945 — nineteen forty five* but *2008 — two thousand and eight*

With **big numbers** we say *and* after *hundred*

e.g.   *178 — one hundred **and** seventy-eight*

   *3,692 — three thousand six hundred **and** ninety-two*

We use the word *point* when we say **decimal numbers**.

e.g.   *3.99 — three point nine nine*

We write **dates** in a different way to how we say them.

e.g.   *19 April — **the** nineteenth **of** April*

2 **Saying numbers**

Practice saying the following numbers. Then write them in words.

1 1.65 billion	**3** 211,090	**5** 1972 (year)	**7** 1997 (year)
2 6.684 billion	**4** 2050 (year)	**6** 5 June	**8** 5.2%

3 Speaking

What do you think will happen to the environment in the future? Look at the following statements. In small groups discuss if they *will definitely happen/will probably happen/may happen.*

1 The amount of forest will increase.

2 The polar ice will continue to melt.

3 The level of the oceans will rise.

4 One day we will only use renewable energy.

5 We will be able to grow crops in the desert.

6 Cars will use renewable fuels.

7 Governments will decide how much energy a family can use.

8 The planet will be less polluted than it is now.

4 Writing

In your groups write a brief report about what you thought about the statements in activity 3. Give reasons for your answers. Present your report to the rest of the class. Do you agree?

INTERNET PROJECT

Calculate your Carbon Footprint

Connect to the Internet and go to www.blackcat-cideb.com or www.cideb.it. See page 52 for how to find the relevant link.

The carbonator can be used to calculate your carbon footprint. But before you do, find out about some of the things which influence it.

1 Work in groups of three. Each person can find out about the influence of travel, home or food on the amount of carbon in the atmosphere. Then tell the other people in your group what you have found out.

2 Now click on 'Carbonator' and calculate your carbon footprint. Compare your results with the other students in your group.

1 Discussing pictures

Look at the pictures below. They all come from different chapters in this book. Work with a partner. Describe what you can see in each picture and tell your partner what you have learnt about it.

2 Planning for the future

Divide your class into four groups. Each group is going to represent one of the natural environments from this book at the UNEP meeting. In the meeting you will all decide how to help the environment in the future.

A   Prepare some information about your ecosystem to explain what the problems are, what you think UNEP should do to help it in the future and why. Each group can use the notes below to help them.

Group A — forests

deforestation   photosynthesis   carbon cycle   global warming
climate   afforestation   sustainable forest management

Group B — oceans

fishing   transport   oil   rubbish   the coast
sustainable fishing   renewable energy   World Ocean Day

Group C — the polar regions

pollution   tourism   industry   oil   governments
greenhouse gases   melt   scientists   Kyoto Protocol

Group D — deserts

desertification   wood   water   crops   global warming
sustainable land management   afforestation
sustainable water management

B   Present your information to the other groups. Now agree on 5 things which UNEP can organise to help as many of the ecosystems as possible.

e.g. Limit how much people can use their car. This will reduce the amount of greenhouse gases in the atmosphere which will help to reduce global warming.

Black Cat Discovery 閱讀系列：

London
倫敦今昔

Gina D. B. Clemen

audio | mp3

商務印書館

Level 1

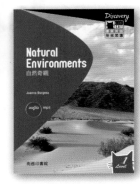

Natural Environments
自然奇觀

Joanna Burgess

audio | mp3

商務印書館

Level 1

Exploring Places
大探險家

Gina D. B. Clemen

audio | mp3

商務印書館

Level 1

American Cities
美國都會

Gina D. B. Clemen

audio | mp3

商務印書館

Level 2

The British Isles
英倫諸島

Derek Sellen

audio | mp3

商務印書館

Level 2

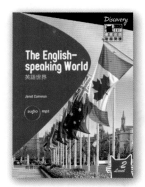

The English-speaking World
英語世界

Janet Cameron

audio | mp3

商務印書館

Level 2

Great British Writers
英國著名作家

Derek Sellen

audio | mp3

商務印書館

Level 1

Level 1 and 2